STANDING BY THE WALL

Books by Mick Herron

Slough House Thrillers

SLOW HORSES
DEAD LIONS
REAL TIGERS
SPOOK STREET
LONDON RULES
JOE COUNTRY
SLOUGH HOUSE
BAD ACTORS

Zoë Boehm Thrillers

DOWN CEMETERY ROAD
THE LAST VOICE YOU HEAR
WHY WE DIE
SMOKE AND WHISPERS

Standalone Books

RECONSTRUCTION
NOBODY WALKS
THE LIST
THIS IS WHAT HAPPENED
THE DROP
THE CATCH
DOLPHIN JUNCTION
STANDING BY THE WALL

MICK HERRON

STANDING BY THE WALL

A SLOUGH HOUSE INTERLUDE

BASKERVILLE

An imprint of JOHN MURRAY

First published in Great Britain in 2022 by Baskerville
An imprint of John Murray (Publishers)
An Hachette UK company

1

A CIP catalogue record for this title is available from the British Library

Paperback ISBN 978-1-399-80708-1
eBook ISBN 978-1-399-80782-1

Typeset in Bembo Std by Palimpsest Book Production Ltd, Falkirk, Stirlingshire

Printed and bound in Great Britain by Clays Ltd, Elcograf S.p.A.

John Murray policy is to use papers that are natural, renewable
and recyclable products and made from wood grown in sustainable forests.
The logging and manufacturing processes are expected to conform to the
environmental regulations of the country of origin.

Baskerville, an imprint of John Murray
Carmelite House
50 Victoria Embankment
London EC4Y 0DZ

www.johnmurraypress.co.uk

To Katie-May and Flossie

'H o.'

The name wasn't so much dropped as thrown from the top of Slough House, and like a snowball finding its target struck Roddy Ho, two floors down, on the back of his neck. He looked up from his screen, senses quivering. He was needed.

'Ho!'

This iteration carried more force; less a snowball, more a localised collapse, as when poor insulation causes a roof to loosen its grip, and its burden of snow hits the pavement with a *whump*. Roddy was already out of his chair, the sleek dynamism of a panther fuelling his every move as he sashayed round his desk, hop-skip-jumped a broken printer, pirouetted past a waist-high stack of pizza boxes, and face-planted on the landing. Damn carpet! He was hearing bells as he picked himself up, and was almost swept away when the third call came: this one a snow tiger cascading down a mountainside, uprooting everything in its path.

'HO!'

Like being summoned by an angry Santa.

On the threshold of Lamb's office he paused, adjusting his expression. Decided to go for quizzical: Spock responding to Kirk's urgent directive with his customary calm, secure in the knowledge that, beneath the necessary camouflage a command structure imposed, they were friends and equals. The captain, subject to the pressures of office, might skirt the boundaries of decorum, but to the practised ear respect was the bedrock of their every exchange. With eyebrow at optimum angle, Ho pushed the door and entered Lamb's den.

'What took you so long, goat-breath? Stop for a dump on the stairs?'

Bantz.

Lamb, Ho noted, was in festive mode, his shoeless feet, currently on his desktop, rejoicing in a pair of

Rudolph socks: a browny-grey reindeer colour, graced at each tip with a bulbous red nose. And on the desk in front of him were scraps of gift wrap it looked like a cross dog had ripped its way free from, the paper's recurring motif – angels and bells, bells and angels – only discernible if you had the kind of mind to reassemble patterns. Roddy was lining up a seraphic chorus, mentally repairing torn wings and cracked casings, before he clocked what had been in the wrapping: a shiny white sheet Lamb was holding, twelve inches by ten, give or take. Any illustration or writing it bore was on the side cradled to Lamb's stomach.

A star-shaped gift tag had fluttered to the floor, attached to a length of green ribbon, on which an actual small bell hung. A message Ho couldn't read was scrawled across the tag, unless a drunk beetle had used it as a shortcut on its way home from an inkwell.

Lamb said, 'Hello? It's like talking to a crash-test dummy.'

'I'm here,' said Ho, briefly contemplating, and as swiftly rejecting, denying the whole dump-on-the-stairs thing, because if Lamb had a fault, it was his occasional inability to put a joke aside before he'd squeezed every last drop out of it. Then again, Roddy reminded himself reasonably, it wasn't everyone had natural comic timing. You had your Roddy types, whose verbal dexterity just naturally brought the sunshine, and then you had your straight men, who milked the laughs by falling flat on their faces. He rubbed his cheek, studded with carpet grit. 'What do you need?'

For a moment, his boss stared off into a middle distance Slough House's walls couldn't contain. 'Christ,' he said. 'The idea that I might need stuff you might supply. Makes me wonder if I took a wrong turn.' Then he pulled his gaze back, and took in the peeling wallpaper, the overflowing desk, the broken slat on the blind covering the dirty window. 'Nah. Living the dream.'

He flipped the sheet he was holding, and held it in the grubby yellow light cast by his lamp.

Which added a sepia tint to the photograph it turned out to be, not that this was a term Roddy reached for. Instead, Roddy just thought: *Old* . . . It was black and white; one of those snapshots of the long-ago that caught, in its subjects' faces, a hint of the melancholy they must feel for a future they'd be too crumbly to enjoy: one in which they wouldn't have to wear baggy suits and hugely lapelled raincoats, or – in the case of the woman – a drab mid-thigh-length dress, with buttons the size of saucers. The three stood in front of a wall, facing the camera; the man in the middle beaming broadly; the woman, on his left, wearing a shyer smile, as if she weren't sure this assignation should be made public. The remaining figure was strangely expressionless, as if caught between two moods, something about him reminding Roddy of someone, he couldn't think who. The woman, meanwhile, was a solid six, maybe seven if she made an effort, but on this showing was all washed out: word to the wise, babe; a touch of the old slap wouldn't go amiss. Anything that gave the sisterhood a leg up got Roddy's vote, and he'd seen enough movies to know that a quick makeover, en route to the lingerie department, could push a six to an eight and a half if you had feminist leanings, and weren't too fussy. But that wasn't happening here, though you could never know for certain about lingerie. As for the man in the middle, he wore a wide-brimmed gangster hat pushed back on his head, as if decked out as an extra for a Roaring Twenties' revival. Both men's shoes were oddly shapeless. Roddy glanced down at his trainers while making this observation: Tommy Hilfiger, dude. Count 'em and weep.

This photo, though. Lamb had been sent it as a Christmas present? Someone didn't like him much. On the other hand, Roddy didn't want to be stepping on anyone's toes whatever their footwear. So he pursed his lips and nodded thoughtfully; eased back a little to adjust his focus, forward to zoom in on the detail. His nodding grew more assured. He stroked his chin and delivered his verdict.

'That's, em, yeah. Art, right? It's, like, yeah. Cool.'

Covered the bases.

Lamb blinked twice, then said, 'It's like Ruskin's in the room.'

'Who's—'

'Shut up. Now, ordinarily the reason I make you run up those stairs is I don't like you and I want you to die. But today, as it happens, I've a job for you.' Still holding the photo so it was facing Roddy, he slapped a meaty hand over the face of the man in the middle, blotting his wide grin. 'I want you to get rid of this guy. Think you can handle that?'

Get rid of this guy . . .

I mean, dude, why not? This was the security service, and if a wet job was on the cards, Roddy was precisely the high-precision tool required. Not that he'd done it before. Had come close a time or two – he could think of a couple of encounters in clubs that would have ended *very* differently if he weren't so self-disciplined – but this, no, this was next level. This was the HoMeister being let off the leash. He could feel his features hardening as he ran down a mental checklist of methods: apparent accident, evident suicide, inappropriate touching. That last wasn't technically an assassination method, but according to Louisa and Ashley, who'd been discussing it in the kitchen last week, it could definitely end in death.

But Lamb was shaking his head. 'Hold your horses, double-oh dickless. If I wanted someone dead, you'd not be the person I'd ask to make it happen. You'd be the person I'd want it to happen to.' He laid the photo on the desk, and reached for a steel ruler Ho dimly remembered as having once been his own. 'Don't worry. Being a deskbound twat might not put you on movie posters, but it suits my purposes, which is a lot more important.'

Roddy allowed a twinkle to show in his eye, to let Lamb know he knew he was kidding. 'So get rid of him how?'

'Like he was never in the photograph. That's the kind of deep-fake mind game you cellar dwellers specialise in, right?' Reaching out with the ruler, he scratched one of his Rudolph noses, which, Roddy now noticed, were peculiarly toe-shaped. In fact, *precisely* toe-shaped. 'Only this time you're on the side of the angels.'

'Yeah, so how—'

'Do I look like I'm interested in hows? I only care about whens. So let's say end of the day, shall we? Gives me something to look forward to, and keeps you out of mischief. Win win.'

'But it's already gone four!'

'What's your point?'

'It's Christmas Eve!'

'Why, did you have plans? No, let me rephrase. Did you have plans that matter? Good.' Lamb pointed with the ruler at the photo, and then, when Roddy had reluctantly picked it up, waved at the door with the same implement. 'Don't make me have to tell you to fuck off.' He beamed, kindly. 'Not on Christmas Eve.'

With grudging tread, Roddy left the room.

Back in his office he scowled. Plans? Of course he had plans. It was Christmas Eve! *Die Hard*, *Die Hard 2* and *Elf*. Unless the others were planning an evening in the pub, which he thought might have happened on previous Christmas Eves, and which he'd allow himself to fall in with if it happened tonight. Spread a little Roddiness. And with every other office worker in the capital heading out for a spot of seasonal insobriety, there was a distinct possibility of the mistletoe effect going viral: Christmas crackers, eager to be pulled! Instead of which here he was, in his office; the streets outside already dark; the dim murmur of conversation in the room above his – who *was* that speaking; they sounded weirdly familiar? – and a way-past boring technical task facing him when he'd been planning on killing the last working hour browsing stocking filler sites. Sometimes, being Slough House's go-to guy was a pain in Ro-Ho's arse.

He paused, checked his scowl, took a selfie. Not bad, actually. But time was ticking on, and he had a job to do.

The photo was smaller than he'd thought; ten inches by eight, with a white border. Laying it flat on his desk, he photographed it, downloaded the result onto his desktop, imported it into a manipulation program the Service carried on its intranet, accessible only by a handful of registered users – yeah, right; big smile, boys, you've been Roddied – and opened it on his main screen. So far, piece of piss.

The next part of the job – making the man disappear – wouldn't stretch him either. Currently, this guy took up the foreground, one arm around the waist of the woman to his left; the other hanging free by his side, with a small but perceptible space between him and the second man, as if one or both were keen to avoid intimacy. The second man's hands were jammed inside his pockets. The look on his face hadn't altered since Roddy first clocked it, that caught-between-two-moods expression, as if he were about to turn one thing or another: nice or nasty. But the first man looked more confident now Roddy had cranked him up, that thirty per cent magnification adding ballast. Not that he needed it. He wasn't beefy exactly, but was well enough built; not the type to impress Roddy, whose wiry frame was the perfect container for the relaxed energy he embodied, but the sort who would make a decent sidekick: not too weighed down by the old brainpower, but able to take a beating. Fancied himself a bit, though. You could tell there was self-satisfaction there, because – dead giveaway – out of his breast pocket poked a jaunty little tongue of handkerchief. Roddy gave an amused shake of the head. Vanity. The vice of mediocrities everywhere.

But no, excising this chump would be the work of minutes. What would take time was joining up the background, leaving no jarring misalignments visible. The background was a brick wall. A grid pattern wasn't the hardest thing to work with, but it meant a lot of straight lines had to meet each other cleanly, and the bricks had to remain of uniform size. The sort of task, in a perfect world, Roddy would hand to an assistant; ideally a blonde with thick-framed glasses she'd remove in pensive moments, tucking the end of one arm behind her lower lip while her eyes went softly out of focus . . . He made a mental note to Google himself some of that, then unglazed his own eyes and activated an outlining tool from a drop-down menu. Using a pencil on his mousepad, he traced a thin white line round the target, highlighting him, making him momentarily brighter, more dazzling, than his companions. Roddy left him hanging like that for a moment, a man from the past in a spotlight cast by the future. Then he pressed a key and *pow*, the figure vanished, leaving behind only a blank space; the nothingness of a background that had disappeared along with him. Making a gun of his fingers, Roddy raised its barrel to his lips, and blew away imaginary smoke.

It was too sudden to be truly awesome, though. The cool way would be a slow melt; the character shimmying away in a *Back to the Future*-style fade-out, taking all his potential, all his impact, with him. Yeah, what would be really ace would be if this guy hadn't just vanished but had ceased to ever be. And what would the ripple effect be like? Roddy wondered. This guy, blinking out of existence: it could cause havoc with the space–time continuum, it didn't take Stephen King to work that out. *Haw*king. Whatever. One moment he's securely rooted in the history of those around him; the next, there's not a pixel of him left. So how would this other pair find it if he just vanished from their lives, and all the things he'd done had never happened? Perhaps they wouldn't have met – perhaps this vanished dude introduced them. Perhaps, without him, they'd have floated away down different paths, leading different lives . . . Roddy shook his head at the philosophy of it all. For an even bigger thought had just landed, one with breathtaking implications – what if *Roddy Ho* were to just vanish; his entire identity, all his adventures, put back in the box like an unstruck match? Talk about the ripple effect. You'd be looking at a tsunami. As he sat there, gazing at his screen with its blown-up image of a trio reduced to a couple, his thoughts shimmied away into a parallel world, one from which the Rodster and all his works had been plucked; a duller, greyer, tone-deaf place, lacking in joy and spectacle. It was hard not to get a little misty-eyed at the prospect, and more on others' behalves than his own. Imagine the heartbreak, he thought. And he allowed himself to do just that; to sit back and picture the world – Slough House – bereft of his presence; touring the ruins as if in the company of a passing angel, who had taken him by the hand to show him how grievously he'd be missed.

'So. Miss me?'

'You've been away? We didn't notice.'

'Except,' said Lech Wicinski, 'there was maybe a tiny uplift in the average IQ?'

He held his finger and thumb a few inches apart, to demonstrate just how tiny.

'And less dicking about,' Shirley said. 'Fewer slammed doors and not so much moody stomping around.'

'Well, coming from you—'

'And a calmer atmosphere,' Louisa agreed. 'Less sexual deprivation in the air.'

'Yeah, that's no longer a—'

'We don't want to hear about it,' said Lech.

'And everyone felt better dressed,' Shirley said.

'So on the whole,' Louisa concluded, 'no, I have to say, it's surprising how well we coped.'

Yeah, thought River. They'd missed him.

Slough House hadn't altered in his absence, or not so he could tell. There was a new occupant, but that was a change often felt least of all: some slow horses had a way of merging with the wallpaper, adopting its rancid pattern, during their first months of tenure; as good a way as any, he supposed, of demonstrating that they belonged here. But once the soul-deadening realisation that this wasn't just a career glitch – that this was their future made solid and served up in one indigestible lump – once that was out of the way, some started to reassert themselves, unless they'd given up by then. Half a year spent fiddling about on the margins of the nation's security – passing your days, say, checking passenger locator forms against NHS records, on the vanishingly small chance that any discrepancy was down to a bad actor's inadequate cover rather than human error, form fatigue or sheer bloody-mindedness – and you'd know whether you were prepared to dig your heels in long-term, or accept that your mental well-being and sense of self-worth depended on finding alternative means of employment, despite the hole in your CV you'd be carrying forever. As far as the Service was concerned, if you bailed on them – even, or especially, if they wanted you to – you ceased to exist.

Of course, remaining on the Service's books when the volume in question was Slough House wasn't that much better a prospect. There were those who'd prefer the clean start, even if that left you way down the ladder, admiring the arses of those who'd made more considered career choices, like accountants or window cleaners or jugglers.

Ashley Khan, the trigger for this line of thought, was leaning against the wall.

'So you're Ash.'

'Uh-huh.'

'How's it going?'

'What is this, a royal visitation? Ask me how far I've come, why don't you?'

'I know exactly how far you've come,' River said. 'We all used to work at the Park.'

'And some of us got screwed over,' she said. 'While the rest of you fucked up.'

'Right. Looking forward to sharing an office with you.'

'Yeah, I've taken your desk, by the way.'

'That's fine,' River said. 'I don't start for a month. Plenty of time to vacate it.'

'That's gonna happen.'

'Then we're both happy.'

Ash stood. 'We'll have lots of time to get to know each other. Don't see any point in wasting this afternoon too.'

She left.

River looked at Louisa, who shrugged. 'You were hardly a bundle of joy either. Back in the day.'

'She's kind of . . .'

'Uptight?'

'I was going to say arsey.'

'I like her,' said Shirley.

'You would.'

'She's over-sensitive,' said Lech. 'Like many millennials. Some of them find punctuation aggressive.'

'Yeah? How'd they feel about a punch in the mouth?'

'Hello, River.'

Catherine Standish had chosen that moment to appear.

Speaking of not changing, here was the touchstone. For as long as he'd known her, Catherine had dressed the same way, moved on the same rails, transmitted on the same frequency: one of measured calm despite the daily aggravations. If Slough House was where you found out what you were made of, River thought, Catherine must have discovered pure titanium below her apparently delicate surface. The clothes she wore might have graced a Victorian doll; her hair, from a distance a grey dull cap, was a wispy fair web where it escaped the slides keeping it tamed. He might have seen her yesterday. He was glad to see her now.

For a moment, he thought she was going to embrace him. That moment – if it actually was one, and not his imagination – passed. But there was warmth in her smile when she asked, 'How are you?'

'Fine. You?'

'No, I meant really.'

'I passed the medical, Catherine. I'm fine.'

And he was, or he was if anybody asked. Anyone bar Sid, that is – she was privy to his nightmares, which were not so much a summoning of the demons his brush with Novichok had tarred him with as a tour of other, earlier griefs. These dreams took him by the hand and led him through his grandfather's house: the rooms, bar one, emptied of possessions; only the study still furnished. In this version, though, it had been ransacked by some furious intruder, its hundreds of books spilled into a heap that might have boiled up from some underground chamber, and he – River – was tasked with putting each back in its rightful place, according to a system ordained by his grandfather, and never revealed to anyone else. Unspecified punishments awaited should he shelve a title wrongly. These dreams, or this single recurring dream, his waking mind interpreted as a mission to restore order where he found chaos, a diagnosis which caused Sid no small amusement. That didn't sound like the River Cartwright she knew. No; his nightmares were random assaults made by his subconscious, just like everyone else's. Deal with it.

The pair of them, though. Sid, River had once bent over on a pavement wet with blood, a bullet in her brain; River, Sid had found on his grandfather's kitchen floor, laid low by a Russian nerve agent. If not made in heaven, their relationship was at least ratified by intensive care.

'When do you start back?'

'Not for a few weeks. Just thought I'd drop in, say hello.'

'That's kind.'

'Wish you all a merry Christmas.'

Louisa said, 'Who are you, and what have you done with River?'

Catherine tilted her head to one side. 'All of us?'

'Haven't decided yet.'

Because sticking your head round Lamb's door to say hello wasn't established practice. He had a way of making you feel unwelcome even when he'd specifically demanded your presence.

'How is he, anyway?' he said.

'Same as ever.'

'That bad?'

Lech said, 'He had an email from HR yesterday, about something called an equality impact assessment.'

'Bet that went down well.'

20

'He emailed back asking how high a window he could use.'

Shirley said, 'If they start checking in with him about our preferred pronouns, he might have a stroke.' The idea obviously pleased her. She looked around. 'So, we going to the . . .' She glanced at Catherine, then away. 'You know.'

Catherine rolled her eyes. 'I'm not about to have a fit of the maidenly vapours just because someone mentions the pub.'

'Yeah, it's just, you're not invited.'

'Of course you are,' Louisa said. 'Shirley's kidding. Aren't you, Shirley?'

'Only if it's understood that, just because she doesn't drink doesn't mean she gets out of buying her round.'

Lech shook his head in what, in a better place, might have been disbelief, but in Slough House was more likely recognition.

'Thanks for the gracious offer, I'm sure,' Catherine said. 'But the pubs will be crowded and I'd rather get home.'

'That was nice,' Louisa said, once Catherine had left the room.

'Why's everyone looking at me?' said Shirley.

River closed his eyes briefly, allowing the familiar discomforts of a broken-backed chair and fractious colleagues to welcome him back to Slough House. But amid the call and response of office life – the jibes and barbs, the occasional harmonies, the inevitable grating discords – a stray thought kept sneaking up on him: *it feels like there's someone missing.*

For the life of him, River couldn't think who.

There were too many moments to recall, too many examples to list, but when you looked back over the last few years – which somehow felt like a decade or more, though obviously wasn't, or they'd all be older – when you did that, no question, it was Roddy Ho holding Slough House together; Roddy whose technical wizardry stopped things going tits up on a regular basis, and kept them tits down the rest of the time. Accessing databases, check. Hacking Service files, check. Verifying the locations of colleagues or minor characters armed with nothing more than their phone numbers, check. Some of this shit bordered on science fiction, and might as well be for all the attention the slow horses paid, as they sat slack-jawed, watching the Rodmeister's hands blur across his keyboard: bish bash bosh – job done. They didn't see the magic. Maybe they had their uses when you needed a blunt object, but for subtlety and grace there was only one Roderick Ho, plus, come to think of it, only one Roderick Ho's car: a Ford Kia, not *exactly* a common sight on the streets. How often had the HoMobile been called into action when a reliable and stylish mode of transport was required? From Wimbledon Common to the woolly wilds of Wales, how many tight squeezes had HotRod's hot rod rescued hapless spooks from? They were utterly clueless, the whole pack. So no, a world from which the Rodster had been erased was a world devoid of happy outcomes for Slough House, and Roddy didn't need a guardian angel to tell him *that*.

Didn't need one to tell him what to do next, either, which was move the two remaining characters in Lamb's photo closer together. And that was Roddy in a nutsack: always bringing the extra noise. Because clearly, with the central figure no longer there, this pair were going to have to shuffle up a bit, otherwise you'd have this weird disconnect going on; an obvious absence keeping them apart. And then, of course, there was the background to be filled in, the wall which was neither obviously new nor evidently old but had to be got right, brick by brick, so that as each pixelated unit slotted into place, you'd have the sense of a world healing itself, coming to terms with the loss of whoever had just vanished . . . Who'd been no one special, Roddy had decided, if all it took to fill the gap he'd left was some CGI brickwork. Compare and contrast with the Roddyless scenario. What kind of grief would be coming Slough House's way, if the world blinked once and Roderick Ho ceased to be? Even leaving aside all the hair's breadth escapes he'd been responsible for – the countless times he'd waved the Roddy wand and pulled a Roddy rabbit from his hat, without which most of the slow horses would be smears across the landscape by now – there'd be the devastating emotional consequences to contend with. Louisa would suffer worst, without even knowing what caused her sense of loss; deep inside her there'd be a Roddy-shaped hole, and she wouldn't even know it. As for the others, well. For Shirley, the Rodster had always been off-limits, of course; be like a donkey expecting to get it on with a thoroughbred, but people couldn't always tell what league they belonged in, and Shirley too would be burdened with a vague awareness of lost possibilities, of never-weres. Ash's chances of a close encounter of the Roddy kind had been higher, making her outlook that much more blighted, but she was young and might get over it. Catherine, though – who looked on Roddy as the son she'd never had – there was no happy outcome there. The best you could hope for was that someone would toss a bunch of flowers into whatever lonely well she ended up in. And Lech Wicinski – well, Lech could fuck off. Even the Rodster's famous compassion had its limits. But for Lamb, for Lamb it would be a case of missing limb syndrome. Every time he had an emergency, every time he had a crucial task, it would be like he was reaching for something that wasn't there, with an arm he no longer had. Imagine the frustration –

'Ho.'

– imagine the grief –

'Ho!'

– imagine the anger –

'HO!'

Roddy hit the printer button and scampered upstairs with his doctored photograph like a man chased by an angel.

Ho, Ho, HO! . . .

Roddy, thought River. How could he have forgotten Roddy?

More to the point, if it was that easy, how come he hadn't managed it years ago?

Must have been the medication he'd been on these past six months. Side effects include: nausea, vomiting, sleeplessness and an eradication of arsewipe colleagues.

The others were deep into discussion about which pub they should head for after work – a formula which rather skated over the notion of how much work was going on – Shirley holding out for a dive on Whitecross Street she claimed did a nice line in craft beers, but whose attractions, the assembled company knew, were more to do with the illicit substance dealing it also specialised in, and Lech and Louisa hoping for somewhere you could be guaranteed a seat, and maybe food. River, meanwhile, was gauging his levels of strength. *I'm fine*, he told everyone, all the time; *I'm fine*, he'd told Sid earlier, when she'd queried the wisdom of this visitation. He wasn't fine. He put on a good show, mostly, but right this moment, for example, he wasn't sure he could stand up without keeling over.

Lech and Shirley were getting loud about what made a good pub good.

'Comfortable seating and no rap on the jukebox,' said Lech.

'Wide range of lagers and flavoured gin,' said Shirley. 'Give the punters a party in their pants.'

'Leaving aside the lager abomination,' Lech said, '"a party in their pants"?'

'What's wrong with that?' Shirley, aggrieved, sounded a lot like a twelve-year-old. 'It's an everyday expression. Like "look before you leap". Or "Prince Andrew denies the allegations".'

While they argued, Louisa rolled her eyes and tapped River on the shoulder. 'You okay?'

'I'm fine.'

She nodded, but not in a way that suggested belief.

To distract her, or maybe just to indicate his grasp on how many slow horses there were, he said, 'Roddy part of this plan?'

'Probably not,' she said, glancing in Lech's direction.

'Hard feelings?'

'Long story,' she said, 'but Roddy ran him over.'

'With a car?'

'With a car.'

'. . . Okay.'

'So things are a bit . . . tetchy.'

River could see how that might be the case.

He heard Ho leaving Lamb's office and briefly saw him through the open doorway as he clumped downstairs. Catherine, he assumed, was in her own office, doing whatever it was she did when she was alone, which probably involved more dedication to tasks in hand than the rest of them managed. Ash was now coming out of her room – River's room, that is, but she'd learn – just across the landing from Louisa's, where Lech and Shirley had reached some at least temporary resolution as to which pub they'd grace with their favours. River had been on office outings before, and knew from experience that any such expedition involving more than two slow horses could end abruptly, with harsh language and the occasional slap. It being Christmas might make a difference, of course – everyone he knew and had ever known, however ill-tempered and misanthropic they might seem the rest of the year, proved themselves to be, deep down, at least twice as bad as that at Christmas.

Louisa was putting her coat on. 'Ready?'

'You go ahead,' he said. 'I'll just say hi to . . .' and he tilted his head to indicate the man upstairs.

'Seriously?'

'I've been pumped way full of drugs this year,' River said. 'I'll probably survive a few minutes in his room.'

Though in truth, he wanted to remain static a little longer, rather than have anyone witness his attempt to stand.

Louisa said, 'You'd have to be on something to even want to make the effort.' She glanced towards the window, as if gauging the weather. It was dark, cold and damp. She named the pub the others had nominated: a big place on the corner at Smithfield Market. 'You'll catch us up?'

'Sure. Probably. I may have to get home.'

'But you're fine.'

'But I'm fine.'

She nodded, and steered the others out, Ash joining them on the landing. River heard them negotiating the stairs; heard the usual tussle with the back door, which stuck in all seasons; heard the final scraping crunch as someone shouldered it into place. Then Slough House was quiet, which meant there was merely the wheezing of the pipes, the groaning of the floorboards, the humming of the light bulbs; and also, as long as he was paying attention, the whirring of computer tomfoolery from Roddy's room below, and the gentle tap of Catherine's feet above, as she crossed the small landing with her customary unhurried pace, and entered Lamb's lair.

Lamb's office, Catherine thought – not for the first time – was a synaesthete's daydream: tobacco, sweat and alcohol, along with the fug of unshared secrets, which had discoloured over the years, adding a rank shade to the spectrum. And under that rainbow Lamb sat, twisting something in his hands, and wearing what the others called his resting bastard face: an expression of wistful viciousness, as if he were remembering a bad turn he'd done someone, and wishing it had been worse. Whatever he was fidgeting with made a small tinkling sound as it dropped to the desk. It was a strip of ribbon, used as gift wrap, to which a small bell was attached.

'You realise that every time a bell rings,' Catherine told him, 'an angel gets its wings?'

Lamb said, 'Yeah, but every time I break wind Tinkerbell punctures a lung. So I figure I'll come out ahead.' He shifted in his seat, and for a moment she feared he was about to demonstrate his organ-deflating abilities. Instead, he reached for a plastic lighter, and dry-clicked it several times. 'What's all the noise downstairs? As if I didn't know.'

'He'll be up soon, I'm sure. To pay his respects.'

'I'd sooner he paid my bar tab. Anyway, his sick leave's still running, isn't it? Shouldn't he be playing shitty sticks in some country retreat, with the other casualty?'

'It's called Poohsticks,' Catherine said.

'Yeah, well, tell him to fuck off. If he's on sick leave, he shouldn't be on Service property. In fact, why not just set the Dogs on him?'

'Because it's Christmas?' She collected the empty mugs from his desk, each half full and rejoicing in at least two drowned cigarette ends. 'Speaking of which, I see Molly sent you a gift.'

'Molly's yanking my chain. It's not the same thing.'

He slumped back in his chair, and into a state familiar to Catherine: one he adopted when pursuing a marathon brood. As a drinker – even if the last glass of alcohol she'd raised to her mouth had been years ago – she recognised the condition: one in which the brooder stared into an oblivion of his or her own making, an oblivion which stared right back, if you let it. Or you could open another bottle, pour another glass. There was a bottle on Lamb's desk now, a detail which barely needed mentioning. A glass too, its surface sticky, a stray hair clinging to its rim.

If she ever needed reminding why she no longer drank, all she needed to do was walk into this room, imagine it her own.

She had known that Molly Doran – Regent's Park's keeper of the files, who guarded her wheelchaired domain like a single-minded Cerberus – was the gift-giver because she had recognised the handwriting on that morning's envelope, sent through the mail rather than the internal courier system, which might indicate a scrupulous awareness of what did and did not count as official Service business, or perhaps just meant that Molly had wanted a fifty per cent chance of it arriving within the fortnight, which was about how often the internal courier made it to Aldersgate Street. That the envelope contained a photograph, Catherine had deduced from the 'Do not bend – contains photo-graph' sticker, and that Lamb had not been expecting it from the distracted mood he'd been in since. He generally marked the festive season with an increase in hostilities. Today he'd barely ventured from his room other than to bellow for quiet or tea four or five times, and, Roddy apart, had invited nobody to suffer his company, preferring to stew in solitude and – one massive coughing fit aside – relative silence. And the silence of the Lamb, more often than not, was an indication of disquiet.

As for the photograph, Catherine hadn't seen it earlier, but it now lay on the desk in front of him, and he was making no attempt to shield it from her gaze. So gaze she did: a couple, in black and white, standing in front of a wall somewhere, years ago. She didn't recognise the woman, though had the vaguest sense that she ought to, but the man was Jackson Lamb.

Who, as if hearing her think his name, stirred and curled his lip.

'Do you want more tea?' she asked, to forestall his asking why she was still there. But he didn't answer.

The photograph was at an angle to her, not far from upside down, but like many a long-time Personal Friday, Catherine could read, absorb and digest printed material from most perspectives, and had little difficulty assessing the image offered. Her initial response was that Jackson cut a surprising figure back when this picture was taken. Not attractive or youthful or fit or healthy, mind; it was, simply, surprising to note that he'd not always been a shambolic mess, but had once been someone you might not bat an eyelid at if they, say, ran up a flight of stairs, or didn't light a cigarette. So this picture was from his war years; not the actual war, obviously; not even the actual Cold War, since that had been over thirty years ago, and the figure in the photo didn't look young enough, but from that period, anyway, when Jackson Lamb had been a warrior, and the enemies he faced flesh and blood, rather than the dim and distant ghosts that bothered him now.

The woman, though . . . She didn't have the look Catherine might have expected from one consorting with the likes of Lamb. Did not, to put it bluntly, look like a professional, by which Catherine didn't mean on the game – or not necessarily on the game – but, rather, in the picture; someone who knew the world Lamb lived in, and had been trained to walk within it too. Instead, she had the appearance of one about to choose a gateway in a riddle. The first would lead to love and fortune, the other to disgrace and loneliness. Catherine preferred images of such women before they'd made that choice, their excitement not yet drowned by apprehension. The dress she wore was eye-catching; its buttons indicating a style classic, though Catherine couldn't put a name to the designer. She wondered if this woman were one of Lamb's dim distant ghosts . . . There was something ghostly about the picture, come to think of it. As if there hovered above the captured pair an unseen spectre, one that had faded into the brickwork, but whose memory remained. Not much given to fey speculation, Catherine dismissed the thought before it could take root, and leave her wondering whether the ghost was friend or foe.

'Are you still here?'

She said, 'I was asking if you wanted more tea.'

'Well don't talk to me when I'm not listening. It's a waste of everyone's time.' As he was speaking, Lamb seemed to notice that his photo was exposed to Catherine's view, and he reached for it and flipped it over. It was on paper, not card, Catherine noticed, and she wondered why the instruction on the envelope had cautioned against bending.

Not caring that he'd know she'd been studying the image, she said, 'Taking a peek into the past?'

'Why would I want to do that?'

'It's the time of year for memories.'

'I don't do memories.'

But they do you, she almost said. Lamb, she felt, would be steamrollered by memories if he let his guard down. Though she no longer speculated, or not often, about what had happened to make him this way, she'd long assumed that when the lists were drawn up of who did what to whom, and at what cost, he'd turn out to be at least as much sinning as sinned against. And that, she knew, could make for sleepless nights.

'Are you still here?' he asked again, and she shook her head. Tea mugs in hand, she closed his door behind her, and paused on the landing, hearing River coming up the stairs. If that photo came from Molly, she thought, Molly must have found it in her archive. Which meant that the image it held wasn't just from Lamb's past, it was from his job. The wall it showed him standing in front of might not be the actual Berlin Wall, but it could easily be a wall in Berlin. He might look like a younger version of himself, but he was pretending to be someone else entirely. And who the woman was was anybody's guess.

I don't do memories.

For a good liar, Lamb came across like a shocking amateur on occasion.

Some minutes after the others had left River stood, and was relieved to find that his legs supported him. There'd been times, as recently as the previous week, when standing upright had proved a bridge too far.

He had reacted to such setbacks with his usual poise.

'There's no point rushing recovery,' his physiotherapist had said.

'There's every fucking point,' River had assured him.

Because becoming whole again, learning to trust his own body, wasn't something he could approach gradually. He had to know that he was back on track, and had to know it soon. Had to know that, by the time he reached his peak again, he wouldn't be over the hill.

'The physio knows what he's talking about,' Sid had said. Repeatedly.

'Yeah, but he's not the one this is happening to.'

'Very adult.'

'It's these sudden . . . weaknesses I can't stand. One moment I'm normal, the next it's like someone's cut my strings. It's as if my body's housing a traitor.'

Sid laughed. 'This is news to you?'

'It's not to you?'

'Well, you've already got a mole on your upper lip.'

'. . . Very funny.'

'River,' she said. 'I get it that you're hoping for a full and fast recovery. You know why I get it? Because I was shot in the head.'

He shook his own head now, remembering that conversation. He and Sid had a good thing happening, he reminded himself. It would be a shame to mess that up by being a dick.

Before he reached the top landing Catherine came into view, cautioning him away with a mug-handed gesture towards Lamb's door and a shake of the head. 'I wouldn't.'

If it was anyone else but Catherine, talking about anyone else but Lamb, River would have pressed on anyway, but that wasn't going to happen here. He stopped on the stairs and gave her a half-wave – 'Bah, humbug, Catherine.' 'Happy Christmas, River.' – then turned and headed back down. He could join the other slow horses in the pub, get used to being in their company once more, or head on home and be with Sid. He decided to head on home and be with Sid. Nothing to do, of course, with not feeling up to a crowded pub. Tip-top form, that was River Cartwright.

He passed Roddy's office, its door half open, and glimpsed Ho at his desk, steering his software towards some distant destination. He was almost at ground level, gearing himself up to tackle the door that never worked, when he stopped, chewed his lip for the best part of thirty seconds, then turned and walked back up. On the first landing he stood for another moment before putting a finger to Roddy's door and pushing gently. It swung open.

When Roddy saw who was invading his space, he scowled. 'Thought you weren't back till next month.'

'I'm fine. Thank you.' He thought about moving further into the room, then decided leaning against the door jamb was a better bet.

A glance around confirmed that Roddy's office hadn't altered much in his absence, beyond having had a windowpane replaced with a grease-stained cardboard mosaic. There was probably a story there, but Roddy was unlikely to reveal it. Roddy wasn't revealing much, in fact, except for an obvious distaste for River's presence, which was a good enough reason, where River was concerned, for prolonging it a while. If his initial motive in returning – a quantum of sorrow that Roddy had been frozen out of the pub trip – had instantaneously morphed into a desire to wind him up, that wasn't a headline-grabbing development. Few benign feelings survived more than a moment or two of Roddy's company. Most would crumble into dust faced with the look he was giving River now.

'What's up with you?' River asked. 'Did they stop making pizza?'

'No, and anyway, what's up with *you*? Did they stop . . .'

River waited.

'. . . putting Novichok on doorknobs?'

'Not soon enough to suit me,' said River. 'What you up to?'

'None of your business.'

'Well of course it's none of my business. I wouldn't be asking otherwise, would I? Haven't you worked out what spies do yet?'

Roddy tilted his monitor, in case River had developed the ability to review a screen's contents from its reverse side. 'Special job.'

'A phrase I often associate with you.'

'For Lamb.'

'What would he do without you? In fact, what would any of us?'

Roddy gave a bored look, as if he'd long plumbed the depths of that particular question.

'You joining the others for a Christmas drink?' River asked.

Roddy looked shifty. 'Why?'

'Because they're going down Smithfield Market. That big place on the corner?'

'Yeah, right.'

'Instead of the one on Whitecross Street.'

'Yeah. Right.'

'I'd hate you to end up in the wrong place.'

Roddy stared, a mixture of doubt and aggression stirring just below his surface.

'Absolute opposite direction,' River said.

'Yeah,' said Roddy. 'Right.'

'Have a good Christmas.'

Roddy grunted.

'I hope you get everything you deserve.'

'And I hope you get a Novichocolate Santa in your stocking.'

That was actually pretty good, thought River.

'And some Novichocolate reindeer.'

But now he was just milking it.

'Don't forget,' he said, turning to go. 'Whitecross Street.'

'You said Smithfield!'

'That's what I meant.'

Down the stairs again, and this time River made it all the way out through the back door, which he was glad no one was around to see him making a meal of. In the yard, its mildewed walls pungent in the cold, he paused while pulling his gloves on and looked back at the building, its only sign of life on this side a dim light on the top floor, leaking through Lamb's blind. He wasn't sure what he'd been expecting from the afternoon – though he'd been glad to see

Louisa and Catherine, and even Lech and Shirley, and even, *even*, didn't feel entirely soiled by having seen Roddy too – but had imagined it would involve encountering Lamb, and felt slightly cheated that it hadn't. But not as bruised, he admitted to himself, as he'd probably have felt if it had. As it was, Roddy's blunt barbs aside, the worst he'd been offered was the new recruit's comment about a royal visitation – ha! The return of the prince . . . Did she imagine he thought he was special? In truth, he had once, probably, but his time as a slow horse had mostly cured him of that. And royalty, no, seriously; this was Slough House, not Clarence House. Which rang a bell, but what did 'Clarence' have to do with anything? And then he remembered Springsteen's saxophonist, and 'Santa Claus is Comin' to Town'. That was it.

It would have been nice if a few flakes of snow started drifting earthwards as he made for the Tube, but they didn't. In ordinary weather for the time of year, River Cartwright joined the crowd heading into the underground, and went back home to Sid.

★

Meanwhile, back in his office, Roddy Ho put the final touches to the photograph, incorporating the further change Lamb had demanded; one which made little sense to him, but who was he to argue? When the boss was ready to share, it'd be Roddy he'd turn to. And he remembered Cartwright's question, What would Lamb do without you?, and supplied the answer he'd come up with earlier: he'd suffer missing-limb syndrome. Which just went to show: when Roddy was right, he was right.

He printed it off, admired it, then took it upstairs, where Lamb had stirred himself enough to pour whisky from the bottle into the glass, and from the glass into his mouth, at least four times since their previous exchange. This one lasted little longer. Roddy put the printout on Lamb's desk and Lamb glanced at it, nothing in his expression changing while he took in the further alteration Roddy had made. Then he picked up his glass, drained it, and set it down again. Something tinkled on his desk when he did so: a plasticky little noise that barely lasted a moment.

'Okay,' he said at last. 'Bah humbugger off, then.'

'Hamburger . . .?'

'Go,' said Lamb, 'away.'

'Oh. Right.' But he paused at the door. 'Merry Christmas.'

'Huh.'

'Doing anything special?'

'I hate to sound like I'm part of the whole snow-flake cancel culture scene,' said Lamb, rearranging his feet on the desk. 'But I'm going to spend most of it pretending none of you exist.'

Roddy went on his way, chuckling.

As he left the building ten minutes later, negotiating the stairs with his usual lithe grace, he ran through the day's events in his mind, satisfying himself that he'd been indispensable once again. Not just the tech wizardry – when had he ever let anyone down in that department? – but the general rolling with the punches, staying ahead of the game, knocking things out of the park, and besting River Cartwright in a verbal duel. Yes, it was beginning to feel a lot like Christmas.

Roddy Roddy Roddy!

Ho ho ho!

It's an awesome life, he thought. Or mine is. And after the briefest of moments in which he allowed himself to pity all those lacking his very special sets of skills, he crossed the road and headed off to Whitecross Street.

Leaving Lamb in his top-floor office, its soft light softened further by a veil of cigarette smoke, so that any observer of a sentimental nature might imagine him a grubby Santa, putting the grot into grotto. But there were no observers, sentimental or otherwise – Catherine having departed, to pursue her own vision of Christmas in her calm and quiet, not unhappy way – so there was no one to flinch when, with surprising suddenness, Lamb swung his shoeless feet to the floor and went barrelling out of the room, entering Catherine's office like a Viking on man-oeuvres. Flakes of plaster fell from the ceiling when the door slammed against the wall; more drifted free as he pillaged desk drawers with the kind of controlled fury that this room alone, of all Slough House, gener-ally provided sanctuary from. Most of what he found he dropped to the floor – reels of sticky labels, cellophane folders, account books, boxes of Biros, treasury tags; all this junk from another era, as if he were trashing a museum installation – littering the carpet with a mess of ancient stationery. But at last he found what he was after, a packet of A4 envelopes, and with this under his arm he stalked back to his domain, leaving the bruised, assaulted room to adjust itself to its new arrangements.

The doctored photograph lay on his desk. Tossing the envelopes aside Lamb crashed into his chair, simultaneously groping for a cigarette and snatching the picture up so he could glare at it from a distance of six inches. For a long while he became still, and whether he was examining the picture for the new truth Roddy's tampering had imbued it with, or looking beyond that to whatever ancient lie it had originally captured, was impossible to say. At last he fumbled in a pocket, produced a plastic lighter, and struck flame on the third or fourth attempt. He held it to his cigarette, and in the following moment seemed ready to apply it to the photograph too, putting a fiery end to whatever speculative journey he was on. But the flame choked of its own accord, and gasped a little, and went out. After maintaining the pose for a few seconds, Lamb gave a flick of the wrist that sent the lighter spinning into the darkness behind him. He laid the photo on the desk again, and sprawled back in his chair, smoking.

It was much later that he left Slough House, and in the meantime, evidently, he'd found a stamp; had evidently found a pen. But tradecraft, perhaps, prevented him from dropping the sealed envelope he now carried into the first postbox he passed, or even the second, and it was still securely under his arm when he arrived on Old Street, which was not his route home. He turned right, his gait steadier than was reasonable given the quantity of Scotch he'd put away, and directed himself towards the far roundabout, its huge video screens releasing visions of Yuletide splendour into the night air, as if the steady beating of mercantile drums might be mistaken for the sound of distant reindeer. Around him the street pulsed with out-of-office life, much of it wearing party hats; there was a constant weaving in and out of the various establishments along the road – eateries, bars and pubs – but Lamb's pace didn't waver as he made his way through the crowds, though at no point did he make as much as elbow contact with those around him. And at some point he dispatched the envelope he was carrying, or at any rate, it was no longer in his possession when he arrived at the roundabout's video windmills and turned and stared back the way he'd come, as if trying to discern the ripples his passage had caused along that crowded thoroughfare, the thousands of tiny accommodations others had made for his passing bulk. But whatever perforations his journey had caused, no trace of them could be seen now. Whether this satisfied him or otherwise couldn't be said, but he stood unmoving for a while, a silent stony figure among a carnival of noisy excess, until at last he jammed his hands in his pockets, and made his way round the huge roundabout, and disappeared somewhere on the other side.

As for the envelope, it re-emerged into the world in the new year, arriving at Regent's Park to be X-rayed, prodded and decreed harmless before being sealed in a suitcase-like plastic shell along with the rest of the day's post and sent down to Molly Doran's floor, where the light was blue and the air chilled to a little below body temperature, which many thought less about the requirements of ageing documents and more about Molly Doran's antipathy to visitors. When she saw it she studied it briefly, then set it aside before attending to the rest of the day's deliveries, and if the envelope weighed on her mind through the hours that followed no sign of this played on her face, which was the usual powdered mask of too much white and too much red, and somehow not enough colour.

But later, once office hours were done, and the lighting on the floor had powered down to a darker blue, she completed one last circuit of her domain, then made her way to her favourite nook in the centre of the labyrinth, one into which her wheelchair slotted as neatly as if it had been designed for the purpose. Removing the envelope from her chair's pocket, she laid it flat on the small table. Christmas was over, and the stamp that Lamb had found, on which an angel blew lustily into a horn, seemed crudely out of place, as if it were summoning revellers to a party long disbanded. That Lamb had affixed it there, she was certain, though his handwriting was never readily identifiable, and this example – she thought – had been written left-handed. But that he would make some riposte to her admittedly provocative gift, she'd more than expected. He was not a man to ignore a challenge. Those who thought him lazy knew only half the story: he put an enormous amount of effort into avoiding activity, true, but he couldn't resist poking at the grit and clinker left by the fires he'd started along the way. Which was what the photograph had been, of course. Grit and clinker. The record of a moment Lamb had gone on to torch.

Molly had found the original down here, among her treasures. She had known it existed, though the file it was from had been stamped [closed] long before her own tenure at Regent's Park had begun. But she also knew that closed files had a way of opening again. The word *Monochrome* was in the air, an inquiry everyone knew would prove fruitless, but which nevertheless had to justify its existence. So wheels were in motion, and Molly knew first-hand that without an effective brake, wheels in motion tended to stay that way. Sending Lamb the photograph hadn't been a warning, exactly. More of a notification.

And now she opened the envelope, to see what response this notification had generated.

If Lamb had intended to cause Molly pain with his tinkering, he would have been disappointed, for when she examined the doctored photograph her face betrayed no emotion; remained a study in professional detachment. The nature of that profession, true, might be open to question, given the over-generous application of powder and paint, but its commitment could not be doubted. For a while all remained still, the only noise the lift passing the floor on its way to the hub. Molly's eyes were clear, alert. And when she at last reacted it was to nod once, as if in appreciation of an opponent's well-considered move, and then to speak aloud with a certain self-conscious playfulness.

'Ho, ho ho,' she said.

Roddy Ho, in fact. Lamb had set his computer munchkin on the job, and the photo he'd returned was both commentary on, and updating of, the original image.

Otis was gone. This was the most obvious emendation; Otis was gone, as if Lamb thought that by obliterating his image, all that he'd wrought in the long-ago could be undone. Except, of course, Lamb knew nothing of the sort was possible – that was clear from the other change he'd had Roderick Ho introduce; one that underlined all the damage that Otis, wilfully or not, had caused. It was a change many would have thought cruel, but as far as Molly was concerned, there'd have been more malice in leaving the image intact. When the original photo had been in her hands, she'd spent an age looking at the third figure, the young woman who both was and was not entirely familiar. It had been like peering down a well, trying to make out a reflection; or staring at someone she'd started a journey with, only to part company when the going got rough. It was impossible to know where the woman in the picture might have ended up, but difficult to imagine it would have been anywhere like Molly's own destination: this wheelchair, this archive, this solitary late middle age. No, in having Roddy digitally erase the figure's legs, Lamb had not intended cruelty; he had, rather, been asserting the inevitability of the here and now. All paths lead to the present. His own story proved that much: all the different histories he'd had, and all had converged on the same ending, as if it were the one he'd chosen for himself. But however deep he'd buried it, sooner or later Lamb would have to face his past. Molly rather thought that time might be coming.

She took one last look at her younger self, her body floating above the ground, and allowed herself to smile. There had been no floating – the pain had been as powerful as gravity – but it had been a long time ago. The woman in the photograph existed no more. Even so, she'd keep this bastardised record of her one-time self. It was of no probative value, of course, but she would preserve it, because an archive was not intended simply to capture the past, it was there to seed future reckonings. In the cabinets all around her consorted ghosts from the past, ghosts from the present, and ghosts from futures yet to come, and the potential consequences of an uncontrolled assembly of any of these made this the most dangerous room in Regent's Park. She'd long been aware of this. It was possible she was the only one who was. But others would find out. You can't seal ghosts up forever.

For the moment, though, she sealed this one back in its envelope. There were several rubber stamps on the desk in front of her, and she collected three of them in her grasp, examining the handles, neatly colour-coded – the red, the green, the black. But there was no real choice to be made. Dropping the other two, Molly held on to the green, and stamped the envelope [pending]. Then laid it flat on the desk before reversing her wheelchair out of her favourite nook, and rolling once more through the dangerous labyrinth of the past, towards the lift.

Coming September 2023

THE
SECRET
HOURS

The Incredible New Novel from
MICK HERRON

PRE-ORDER NOW